The Golden Book of
MONKEYS, APES,
and Other Primates

By Maida Silverman
Illustrated by James Spence

Consultants:
Mark Rosenthal, Curator, Mammals, Lincoln Park Zoo, Chicago
James G. Doherty, General Curator, Bronx Zoo, New York

A GOLDEN BOOK • NEW YORK
Western Publishing Company, Inc., Racine, Wisconsin 53404

LET'S MEET THE PRIMATES

For hundreds of years primates were mysterious creatures. Very little was known about them, so tales were told of weird nighttime creatures with shining, ghostly eyes, and beasts that cried like human babies. Stories spread about little creatures with snakes for tails, and about others that were huge, hairy giants bigger than men!

In the past hundred years people have learned more about primates than was known about them in the past hundred centuries! They have discovered facts that are just as exciting as all the old stories about primates. This book will take a close look at three major primate groups: prosimians, monkeys, and apes. Each major **group** contains different **types** of primates. And each type of primate may be further divided into different **kinds** of primates. For instance, in the major group of monkeys, there is a type of primate called the guenon (GWEE-non). Taken further, the vervet (VER-vet) is a kind of guenon.

gorilla (ape)

bushbaby (prosimian)

All primates are mammals. This means they have backbones, warm blood, and hair on their bodies. They have lungs that breathe air and they give birth to babies that drink their mother's milk.

Primates are the only mammals that have flat nails instead of claws. They also have eyes that face forward. Many animals have one eye on each side of the head. Eyes that face forward enable primates to judge depth and distance better than any other animal.

Sixty million years ago the first primates were scampering around in tree branches while dinosaurs walked on the ground. These early rat-sized primates were called Adapidae (a-DAP-a-day). Now let's meet the fascinating primates of today's world.

woolly monkey (monkey)

PROSIMIANS, THE "PRE-MONKEYS"

Long ago, prosimians lived all over the world, in North and South America, Europe, Africa, and Asia. Gradually, over millions of years, the early prosimians died out. Scientists have learned this from fossils. A fossil is the remains of a plant or an animal that is preserved in the rocks of the Earth. Fossils of more than sixty prosimians no longer in existence have been found in all the places just mentioned.

The prosimians of today live in the tropical jungle forests and dry, shrubby places of Asia and Africa. Most of them live in trees, where they sleep by day and look for food by night. This way they do not have to compete for food with the stronger apes and monkeys, who feed by day and sleep by night.

potto

Prosimians like a variety of foods. The mouse-sized tarsier (TAR-seer) eats only insects, while other prosimians eat a mixed diet of leaves, fruit, gummy tree sap, bugs, and even small lizards!

Prosimians can see very well at night. They have large, round eyes that contain a thin sheet of tissue called a tapetum (ta-PEE-tum). The tapetum helps a prosimian see better in a dark tropical forest.

In addition to their large eyes, prosimians have large ears that can catch the faintest sounds. Prosimians can hear the tiny noises made by insects, which helps them to catch and eat their prey. Their remarkable hearing also helps prosimians to avoid being caught and eaten by other animals, such as snakes.

dwarf lemur

tarsier

mother carrying
young bushbaby

SOME AFRICAN PROSIMIANS

Shy pottos (POT-toes) and bushbabies are types of prosimians that live in the forests of Africa. They tend to hide among the bushes and trees, away from predators and other creatures. There are six different kinds of bushbaby and one kind of potto.

The bushbaby got its name from its habit of living in the forest, or "bush," and from its cry, which is like that of a human baby. The Senegal bushbaby has fluffy yellow-brown fur on its upper body. While the body of this appealing little animal is only six inches long, its tail is nine inches long! A mother carries her tiny mouse-sized baby in her mouth, much as a mother cat carries a kitten.

A potto likes to hang upside down from a tree branch and can stay this way for hours at a time. Before it is old enough to find its own food, a baby potto pulls food—leaves, fruit, or a beetle—from its mother's mouth and eats it. The mother never objects. This is the way a baby potto learns what is safe to eat.

10

SOME ASIAN PROSIMIANS

Lorises (LOR-ris-is) and tarsiers are prosimians, too. They live in the forests of Asia and Indonesia. Like their African cousins, they are shy and hard to find. There are three different kinds of lorises and three different kinds of tarsiers.

The loris is famous for its slow-motion crawl. Like its potto relative, it loves to hang upside down from a tree branch. A loris never lets go of one tree branch until it has a firm grasp on another one. However, this slow, careful prosimian can pounce with amazing speed on an insect it wants to eat!

The little tarsier is not much bigger than a hamster. Its tail is almost three times as long as its body. A tarsier cannot see very well what is going on to the side and behind it. To make up for this, a tarsier can move its head around to its back. The tarsier's head then looks like it is on backward!

slow loris

tarsier

mouse lemur

aye-aye

THE AMAZING LEMURS OF MADAGASCAR

Madagascar is an enormous island off the east coast of Africa. It was once part of the African continent, but about 40 million years ago it separated from the rest of Africa and took the ancestors of today's lemurs (LEE-merz), another type of prosimian, with it.

There are more than twenty different kinds of lemurs. Many years ago French explorers to the island gave lemurs their name, which means "ghost." The explorers probably decided on this name because of the lemurs' almost-human, moaning cry and their eyes that shine in the dark.

Despite the meaning of their name, lemurs are not at all harmful. They are active, playful, and gentle. One kind of lemur, the aye-aye (eye-eye), probably deserves the prize as the most peculiar prosimian. Its red eyes are set in its catlike face, which is topped with large, pointed ears. Natives on the island once thought that these strange-looking animals were the reincarnated spirits of their own dead relatives!

12

indri

Madagascar is also home to the world's smallest primate, the mouse lemur. It weighs only two ounces and is about the size of a mouse. Mouse lemurs mainly eat insects, but they also enjoy fruit and flowers.

The biggest lemur in Madagascar is the indri (IN-dree). A full-grown male can weigh almost twenty pounds, and is almost three feet long. With its round, furry ears and fluffy fur, an indri looks very much like a teddy bear. The long, wailing cry of an indri can be heard for miles.

Another active lemur, the ring-tailed, is the size of a pet cat. It races with ease along tree branches and on the ground. The ring-tailed lemur waves its long tail constantly, using it like a flag to signal its whereabouts to others in its group.

TWO MONKEY GROUPS

Monkey is the word most commonly—and mistakenly—used to describe the wide variety of primates. Not all primates are monkeys. However, of the more than three hundred different kinds of primates, over two hundred are monkeys. This is more than all the other primates put together!

There are two major monkey groups: New World monkeys and Old World monkeys. New World monkeys are found in the tropical rain forests of South and Central America. They are called New World monkeys because when the Americas were discovered by explorers from Europe nearly five hundred years ago, they called these lands the New World.

Where did these New World monkeys come from? It's a mystery we have not yet solved. Some scientists think that monkey ancestors, now extinct,

ouakari

cotton-topped marmoset monkey

squirrel monkey

came down from North America at least 60 million years ago. Fossil remains show that wild monkeys were once common in North America, but they died out long ago.

Old World monkeys are found in Africa and Asia. Most kinds of Old World monkeys are larger, stronger, and more intelligent than New World monkeys. Some of them live in the trees in tropical forests. Several kinds of African monkeys are also at home in big, open grasslands called savannas.

Many other Old World monkeys spend time on the ground as well as in the trees. Some are even able to live near people. They raid gardens for fruit and even poke through rubbish heaps for something delicious to eat.

All New World monkeys, on the other hand, spend their lives in the trees, eating leaves, fruit, seeds, and buds. They also enjoy eating insects, spiders, and tree snails, and get their water from wet leaves.

Most monkeys—both Old and New World—sleep high up in the trees, where they are safe from larger animals that might eat them.

DeBrazza's monkey

owl monkey

Schmidt's white-nosed monkey

proboscis
monkey and baby

A BABY PRIMATE GROWS UP

All primates are born into a group. It may be a family group, consisting of a mother, father, and siblings, or a group consisting of males and females of all ages who live together most of the time.

Primate babies often have a distinguishing feature which tells others in the group that they are young and need special attention and protection. For instance, an infant may be lighter in color than its parents. A baby gorilla has a white tail tuft. Baby gorillas can climb all over adults without being chased, which they would be if they lacked this mark of childhood. An adult gorilla would not be allowed to behave this way.

All primate mothers are devoted parents. They feed, care for, and protect their babies as they grow. They carry them almost all the time.

Primate babies have the ability to learn by watching adults and copying what they do. When a baby is old enough to eat solid food, it begins by eating the bits its mother drops. This is how the baby learns what is safe to eat. The baby also learns how to move without falling and how to recognize different kinds of primate calls.

As soon as a baby is strong enough, it spends a lot of time playing with others its own age. Playing games together helps young primates learn important things. By playing, youngsters learn to respect others and get along with them. Little by little, a baby primate grows up and learns to take its place in the group and in the world.

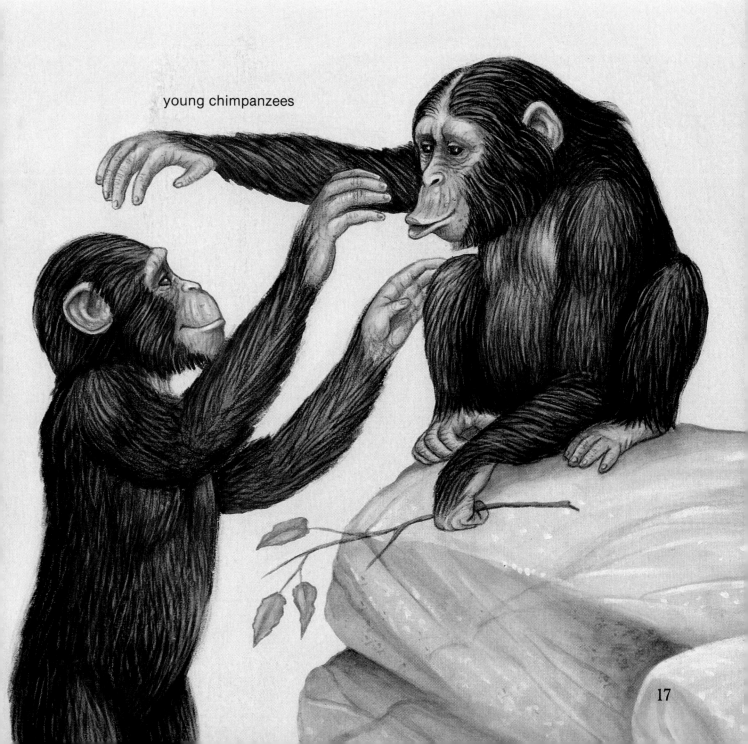

young chimpanzees

17

DIFFERENT KINDS OF
NEW WORLD MONKEYS

Some New World monkeys have long tails that can grasp branches and pick up objects. This type of tail is called a prehensile tail and it has a pad of bare skin on its underside that is as sensitive as the palm of a person's hand.

Woolly (WOOL-lee) monkeys have prehensile tails. Baby woollies love to hang by their tails and swat each other with their free hands. They fight and wrestle and open their mouths wide, which is a signal that it's all meant in fun.

The saki (SAK-ee) has shaggy fur and a long, thick tail that cannot be used for grasping things. But this hairy monkey is the best leaper of all South American monkeys. When chased by a predator, a saki confuses its enemy by alternately leaping very fast and then suddenly stopping.

woolly monkeys

saki monkey

Some New World monkeys are very vocal. One kind of monkey is even called the howler (HOW-ler). The howler is a big monkey, weighing sixteen to twenty pounds. A hollow place in the howler's large lower jaw allows it to make incredibly loud noises that echo through the jungle at sunrise.

The owl-faced douroucouli (DO-ro-COO-lee), or owl monkey, probably does not appreciate these early morning calls since it is the world's only monkey that is active at night. It is ready for bed when the other monkeys are getting up!

Titi (TEE-tee) monkeys use their voices to defend their territories from other titi families. Many noisy voice battles take place throughout the jungle.

The father titi monkey is the most devoted of all male monkey parents. The mother titi monkey nurses the baby but it is the father who carries and protects it. Titi families often sleep together with their tails wrapped around each other.

red howler monkey

19

THE PIGMY MARMOSET: THE WORLD'S SMALLEST MONKEY

At home in the rain forests of the upper Amazon River in South America, the pigmy marmoset (PIG-me MAR-mo-set)—the world's smallest monkey— lives in family groups of five to ten.

The hamster-sized marmoset is an expert at hiding from enemies like big snakes and birds of prey. The pigmy marmoset's brown fur, flecked with lighter and darker shades of brown, helps to make it nearly invisible among light and dark leafy branches. To further confuse an enemy, the marmoset can either scurry along and then suddenly stop, or move so slowly into the foliage that it looks as if nothing is moving.

Pigmy marmosets have also managed to adapt to the presence of man. They can live in the clusters of trees that often remain after their forests have been cleared by man. Marmosets have also ventured into farmers' pastures to look for grasshoppers, something they especially like to eat.

THE LION TAMARIN: AN ENDANGERED MONKEY

Four hundred years ago huge tropical forests grew along the Atlantic coast of what is now Brazil. These forests were home to a little monkey called the lion tamarin (TAM-A-rin). With its beautiful golden-orange mane of fur, it is easy to see how this monkey got its name.

Such bright fur makes lion tamarins easy pickings for eagles and other animals that like to eat them. Fortunately, lion tamarins can move with amazing speed to get away from predators.

Despite their running abilities, lion tamarins are in danger of vanishing forever. They were once much collected and sold as pets. Their numbers have been further reduced due to the destruction of their forests by humans.

Some people are trying hard to save the lion tamarin. It is now illegal to sell them as pets, and scientists are breeding lion tamarins and returning them to the wild, where it is hoped they will live and raise their young.

DIFFERENT KINDS OF OLD WORLD MONKEYS

Like the lion tamarin, some Old World monkeys have also become endangered by the acts of humans. The gentle douc langur (DOOK LAN-gur) monkey of Southeast Asia, for instance, is among the most beautiful primates in the world, with its unusual almond-shaped eyes and brightly colored fur. During the Vietnam War, much of its jungle home was destroyed. It is now hard for the douc langur to find the leaves, fruit, and flowers that make up its diet. This situation could threaten the existence of the entire douc population.

Old World monkeys are just as lively and varied as New World monkeys. Guenons are the most common monkeys in Africa. There are about sixty-seven different kinds of guenon.

vervet monkey

rhesus monkey

The best-known guenon is the vervet, a monkey whose legs are longer than its arms. When a vervet runs along tree branches, it holds its tail straight out to help it keep its balance. Unlike New World monkeys, Old World monkeys do not have prehensile tails (tails that grasp or pick things up).

Most Old World monkeys have thick pads of hairless skin on their bottoms. These pads act like cushions that allow the monkeys to sit comfortably when they rest or eat. Many Old World monkeys also have facial cheek pouches where they can store food to be eaten later.

Proboscis (pro-BOS-cus) monkeys live along jungle rivers in Borneo and are good swimmers. The adult male proboscis monkey probably has the strangest face of any monkey. A large, pear-shaped nose hangs down over its mouth. No one knows why proboscis monkeys have such odd noses, or what they are useful for, besides smelling.

The rhesus (REE-sus) monkey, a member of the macaque (ma-KAK) family, is perhaps the most intelligent monkey. Rhesus monkeys have been used for important scientific research. A rhesus monkey was the first primate space traveler.

proboscis monkey

douc langur

THE SNOW MONKEYS' WINTER TREAT

Snow monkeys live on the Japanese island of Honshu, farther north than any other monkey, ape, or prosimian. They are called snow monkeys because winters in Honshu are long and cold and deep snowdrifts cover the ground. The trees are bare for six months at a time, leaving only tree bark and seeds for the monkeys to eat. The snow monkeys huddle together and depend on their thick fur to keep out the cold.

During the winter of 1963, scientists studied a group of snow monkeys that lived near a hot spring. A hot spring is a place where water, warmed by heat deep inside the Earth, bubbles to the surface and forms a pool. One day the scientists were amazed to see a two-year-old female snow monkey jump into the water!

It wasn't long before other young monkeys joined her. Soon the whole group, youngsters and adults, was enjoying a winter treat.

The monkeys liked to test the water by dipping a hand or foot in it. Soon they were dog-paddling around and even diving underwater. A few monkeys liked to sit in the water, with only their heads sticking out, enjoying the delightful warmth.

The snow monkeys had even figured out when to come out of the water. They did this before sunset so their fur would dry in the sun. After sunset, in the colder nighttime air, the wet monkeys could have frozen to death.

THE MANDRILL

Baboons (bah-BOONS) are large monkeys that can weigh from twenty-five to eighty pounds. They have narrow, doglike muzzles and short tails. Mandrills (MAN-drills) are baboons that live in the jungles of West Africa. Mandrills are quite noisy. They can make deep grunting sounds and loud crowing calls.

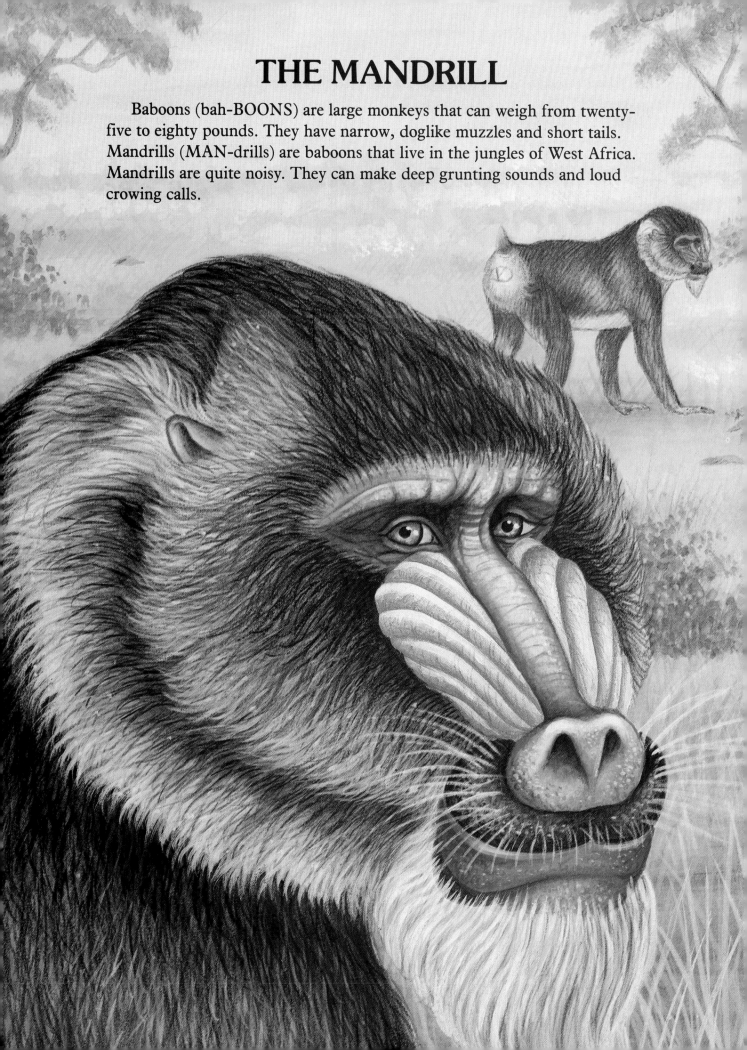

An adult male mandrill will never be mistaken for any other kind of monkey. He has a gaily colored face: a bright red nose, electric-blue striped cheeks, and a fluffy beard of orange and white fur. A male mandrill's bottom is so brightly colored, it looks like this monkey accidentally sat down on an artist's paint box!

A mandrill sometimes shows its long, sharp canine teeth by slightly lifting its lips. This makes the mandrill look very fierce, but it doesn't mean the mandrill is planning to bite. It's the mandrill's way of welcoming someone it knows. Mandrills are actually gentle plant eaters who also enjoy snacks of termites and ants. They will not attack unless they feel threatened by a predator, most probably a leopard.

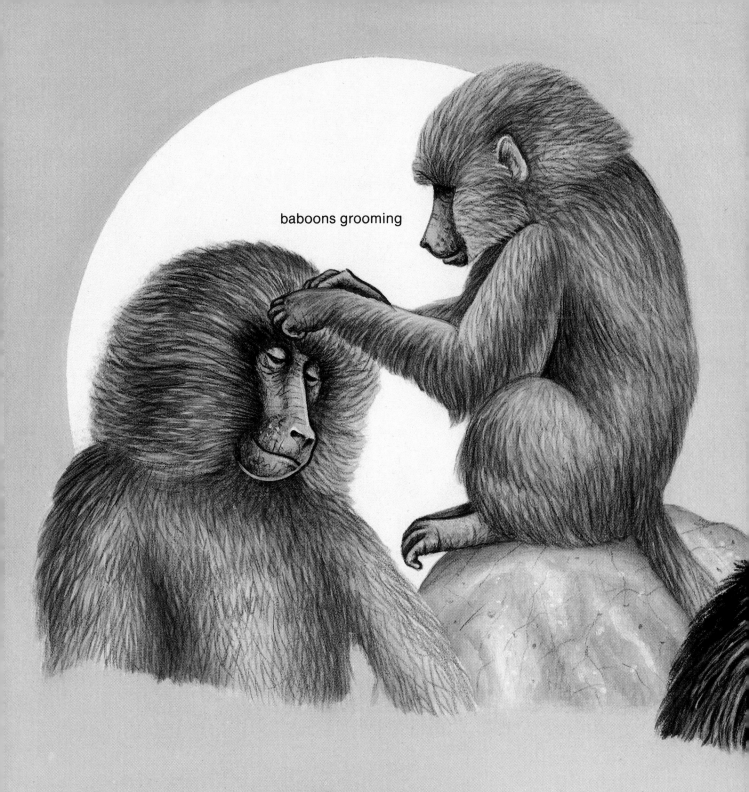

baboons grooming

GROOMING

Monkeys in the zoo are often seen picking through each other's fur. People who watch this wonder what the monkeys are doing. Do they have fleas?

Monkeys examine each other's fur in an activity called grooming. Grooming is the way monkeys and apes keep clean, but it is more than just that. It relaxes and soothes them and helps to develop the good feelings and strong ties that keep families together. Mothers groom their babies, and young monkeys make friends with older ones by offering to groom them.

28

grooming begins
with a touch

chimpanzees

A monkey who wants to be groomed comes up to another monkey and offers a part of its body—perhaps an arm or a leg. The other monkey hardly ever refuses. It grooms the first monkey by parting the fur and picking out bits of dirt, dead skin, and perhaps even tiny bugs.

Grooming takes a long time. Each part of the skin is carefully and thoroughly cleaned. Lots of attention is given to the monkey's head. When one monkey finishes grooming another, they change places.

chimpanzee

orangutan

FASCINATING FACTS
ABOUT APES

More than four hundred years ago travelers returning to Europe from
Africa brought back stories of incredible monsters—strange, hairy "animal-
men" that lived in the jungles and were very dangerous, attacking people and
even killing them.

These tales were so exaggerated that for a very long time, no one really
knew what was fact and what was fiction. Gradually, explorers and scientists
learned that these weird creatures were really gentle animals—apes—and not
monsters at all.

There are four different types of apes. The biggest three—gorillas,
orangutans (O-RANG-a-tans), and chimpanzees—are called the great apes.
Gibbons (GIB-bons), because they are smaller, are called the lesser apes.

gorilla

gibbon

All apes have long, strong arms, broad chests, short legs, and no tails. The big toe of an ape's foot is thumblike. This means an ape's feet can grasp things the way a human's hands can, and is also why an ape's feet are good for climbing and holding on to things. And, like a human's hands, an ape's hands have their own set of fingerprints!

Apes often move from tree to tree by swinging among branches. Sometimes an ape walks upright, but it really can't take more than a few steps this way.

Apes differ from monkeys and prosimians in several ways. They are the largest primates, have the biggest brains, and are also smarter than either monkeys or prosimians. Apes take longer to grow up than monkeys and prosimians do, but they also live longer. A gorilla can live to be more than fifty years old.

GIBBONS

Gibbons are the playful acrobats of the jungle. There are six different kinds of gibbons and they all live high among the trees of southeast Asian jungles.

Adult gibbons weigh from five to thirteen pounds, and have light bones, extremely flexible shoulders, and long, slender arms and fingers. Gibbons are more graceful and agile than any monkey or any other ape.

Gibbons can move so quickly that people watching them bounding through the trees think they must be flying. This is because gibbons can travel at speeds of up to an amazing thirty miles per hour!

With their legs and feet tucked up under their bodies and out of the way, gibbons move from branch to branch. This swinging, arm-over-arm movement is called brachiation (BRAK-ee-a-shun). A gibbon can leap more than twenty feet, going rapidly from tree to tree, without falling.

Gibbons mate for life and live in family groups that consist of parents, an infant, and two or three youngsters. A gibbon baby is cared for devotedly by its mother. She carries it everywhere in her arms and sometimes it clings to the fur of her stomach. When a gibbon is about seven years old, it is considered an adult and it goes off to find a mate of its own.

Each gibbon family has a tree or group of trees that it defends against other gibbons by loud "singing." The parents usually sing a duet, with the female gibbon taking the biggest role.

As the sun rises and again when it sets, gibbon music begins. These noisy competitions are used by gibbon families to announce their territory—the place where they eat, rest, and sleep.

One kind of gibbon, the siamang (SEE-a-mang), has a sac of skin at the base of its throat. This sac swells like a balloon and helps to make the siamang's call the loudest of all.

"MAN OF THE WOODS"
—THE ORANGUTAN

Orangutan means "man of the woods" in the Malay language. There is only one kind of orangutan, and it lives only on the Asian islands of Borneo and Sumatra.

For centuries, the people who lived on these islands thought orangutans were really humans—men who had gone to hide in the remote jungles so they would not have to work!

But while orangutans did not turn out to be lazy men, they did turn out to be the slowest-moving apes. Adult orangutans are quite large. An adult male can weigh more than three hundred pounds and be up to five feet tall. Because of their weight, orangutans prefer to move slowly and carefully from tree branch to tree branch.

The orangutan's only real enemy is man. Hunters and poachers capture them to sell them, even though it is illegal to do so. In places where orangutans live, the trees of their forest home are being cut down to make way for farms and grazing land for cattle.

High up in the trees, a mother orangutan will hold branches together so that her baby can safely cross a gap between two trees. (An adult orangutan has a seven-foot armspan, which is longer than the height of most adult humans.) But if the gap is too wide to close with her arms, the mother will use her body as a bridge for the baby to walk across.

An orangutan mother lives with her baby because the baby needs care and protection, but other adult orangutans live alone. Orangutans are the only primates who do not live in small family groups or large troops. When a youngster reaches the age of about seven, it usually goes off on its own.

Orangutans love to eat fruit, especially figs. No one understands how, but orangutans know when various fruits they like to eat are ripe. An orangutan will travel great distances and find that several others have also arrived at the same tree for a feast. Once there, these shy and peaceful primates will ignore each other and eat their fill—together, but apart.

CHIMPANZEES

Until about one hundred years ago, people thought chimpanzees were just small gorillas. Today we know they are a separate type of ape. There are two kinds, the common chimpanzee and the pigmy chimpanzee, or bonobo (BON-a-bo). The bonobo is the smaller of the two and very little is known about its life in the wild. Chimpanzees, or chimps, live in the tropical forests and grasslands of West and Central Africa.

Chimpanzees live in groups of about twenty chimps. Within large chimpanzee groups, smaller bands form that constantly change in size. There are young all-male bands and mixed bands of males and females. There are mother-baby bands that consist of three or more mother-baby pairs. There are even lone males and females. Different bands mingle as they all search for food.

Male chimps are sometimes interested in a newborn infant, but a chimpanzee is raised by its mother. The mother carries the baby in her arms and never parts with it. If the baby tries to creep away, the mother will gently retrieve it. The mother plays with the baby and comforts it when it is unhappy or scared.

Baby chimpanzees drink their mother's milk. When a chimpanzee is about six months old, it begins to eat solid food and play with other youngsters. A chimpanzee is full grown at about thirteen years of age and can live to be fifty years old.

Chimpanzees use facial expressions and sounds to show many different feelings. A chimp shows a variety of emotions by opening its mouth, including fear. An excited chimp purses its lips and hoots. When two chimps meet after being separated for a while, they hug, kiss, and pat each other on the back.

CHIMPANZEE INTELLIGENCE

Chimpanzees are very smart primates. In the wild, they can make and use simple tools. A chimpanzee who wants to eat termites uses a twig to catch them. The chimpanzee pulls all the leaves off the twig and inserts it into the termite mound. When the twig is removed, it will have termites clinging to it, and the chimpanzee will have a meal!

In laboratories, scientists working with chimpanzees have been amazed by the chimps' abilities. They can learn, memorize, remember, and make use of what they have learned.

At a primate-study center in the United States, a group of chimps learned to use vending machines and colored coins provided for them by the scientists. The chimps quickly realized that, depending on their color, the coins produced larger or smaller amounts of food from the vending machine. When they had enough to eat, some chimps saved their coins for later use. Others, who had spent all their coins and were still hungry, begged for coins from the chimps who still had some!

GORILLAS—
THE GENTLE GIANTS

Although they are huge and scary-looking, gorillas are actually very peaceable and spend almost all their time on the ground, eating plants and resting. Females and youngsters build sleeping nests in trees. Males make sleeping nests on the ground.

There are two kinds of gorillas, the lowland and the mountain gorilla. Lowland gorillas live on the ground in the hot, damp jungles of Central Africa. Mountain gorillas live at levels of as high as 10,000 feet in the mountain forests of Central Africa. Mountain gorillas have longer, thicker fur than the lowland gorillas because the nighttime mountain air can become very cold.

An adult male silverback gorilla is the world's largest primate. He can weigh more than four hundred pounds and stand almost six feet tall. Silverbacks get their name from the large patch of silver-gray hair that covers their backs. These silver hairs start to appear when the gorilla is about thirteen years old.

All gorillas travel in groups of five to thirty young males and females. Each group is led by a silverback who protects them and decides where they will eat.

Many years ago explorers who visited Africa brought back terrifying stories about gorillas. They called them forest demons and dreadful monsters. These people had probably seen or heard about a gorilla's display of anger, without understanding it.

A male silverback scares off an enemy—perhaps another male gorilla—by performing an impressive display. First he hoots and growls. Next he rises to his full height. He roars and pounds his chest. Then he charges—first on two feet, then on all fours. He stops and thumps the ground with his hands.

This performance usually sends an enemy running. If it does not, the gorilla might then attack. This misunderstood behavior gave the gorilla its fearsome reputation, which later became the model for the frightening giant ape in the movie *King Kong*. This reputation is completely undeserved, for gorillas are the gentlest primates of all.

In laboratories, scientists have found gorillas to be very intelligent. In a famous experiment, a gorilla named Koko learned to use sign language to express her feelings and ideas. Koko can joke, answer questions, and even tell a lie—all in sign language.

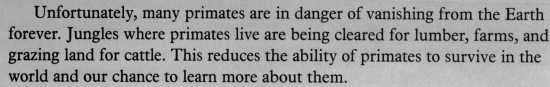

Unfortunately, many primates are in danger of vanishing from the Earth forever. Jungles where primates live are being cleared for lumber, farms, and grazing land for cattle. This reduces the ability of primates to survive in the world and our chance to learn more about them.

Fortunately, people are aware of the need to protect primates and other animals. They are an enormous and important part of life on Earth and have been for millions of years.

In many countries where primates live, large areas of land have been set aside as national parks and reserves. The animals can live protected and undisturbed there. To help these countries maintain and protect the animals, funds are raised and donated by people from all over the world.

There are many organizations that are helping to save the primates. They support research that helps scientists learn more about primates. They also support efforts to protect the places where primates live. To find out what scientists and others are doing and what you can do to help, write to:

The Primate Specialist Group
c/o Conservation International
1015 18th Street NW
Washington, DC 20036

Wildlife Conservation International
The New York Zoological Society
185 Southern Boulevard
Bronx, New York 10460

Primarily Primates, Inc.
P.O. Box 15306
San Antonio, Texas 78212

Wildlife Preservation Trust, International
34th Street and Girard Avenue
Philadelphia, PA 19104
(This organization has a club, The Dodo Club, that you can join!)

INDEX